Mr Bear's
irthday

ORCHARD BOOKS
338 Euston Road, London NW1 3BH
Orchard Books Australia
Level 17/207 Kent Street, Sydney, NSW 2000
First published in 2010 by Orchard Books
First published in paperback in 2011
ISBN 978 1 40830 460 0
The right of Debi Gliori to be identified as the author and illustrator
of this work has been asserted by her in accordance with the Copyrights,
Designs and Patents Act, 1988.
A CIP catalogue record for this book is available from the British Library.
1 3 5 7 9 10 8 6 4 2
Printed in China
Orchard Books is a division of Hachette Children's Books,
an Hachette UK company.
www.hachette.co.uk

MR BEAR'S
BIRTHDAY

Debi Gliori

ORCHARD BOOKS

"Happy birthday, Daddy!" said Small Bear.
"Are you very old?"
"Not very," said Mr Bear.
"Will you have thousands of candles
on your cake?" asked Small Bear.

"Not thousands,"
said Mr Bear,
heading downstairs.
"Just a few hundred."

In the kitchen, Mrs Bear was busy feeding
Baby Bear.

"Happy birthday, dear," she sighed. "I haven't
baked you a cake because we've run out of flour."

"I'll go and get some right now," said Mr Bear.
"I love birthday cake."

"I'll come with you," said Small Bear,
following Mr Bear out of the door.
"Haven't you had any birthday cards yet?"
"Not yet," said Mr Bear,
"but maybe the postman
will bring me some."

Poor Mr Bear. Mr Rabbit-Bunn had nothing exciting in his mailbag.

"Never mind," said Mr Bear. "It's a lovely day for a birthday. Who needs birthday cards?"

No sooner were the words out of Mr Bear's mouth than the sky turned grey and it began to rain. Mr Bear lifted Small Bear onto his shoulders and ran for cover.

Inside the flour mill,
they found Mr Grizzle-Bear
frowning over a little bit of
bent metal.

"It's not my lucky day today,"
he said. "I'm afraid the mill
isn't working because this cog is broken."

"It's Daddy's birthday today," said Small Bear.
"We need flour for his cake."

"I need a cog for my windmill," said Mr Grizzle-Bear,
"otherwise I won't be able to grind any flour."

"I need a birthday cake," said Mr Bear. "I'll go
and get you a cog straightaway."

"Poor Daddy," yawned Small Bear.
"No cake, no birthday cards, no flour . . . "

"No problem," said Mr Bear. "Mr Hoot-Toowit
will have a cog in his tool shop, and then
Mr Grizzle-Bear will be able to fix his windmill,
and we'll be able to grind some flour and before
we know it, we'll be eating your mummy's
wonderful birthday cake."

"Are we there yet?"
yawned Small Bear.
"I'm hungry."

It was a long way to Mr Hoot-Toowit's
tool shop, but before they got there, they
could hear Mr Hoot-Toowit shouting.

"Stop thief!
That's mine, not yours . . .
Put it back, you thieving magpie."

Inside the tool shop, Mr Bear groaned.

"Was that the only one you had?"

"The very last cog," Mr Hoot-Toowit sighed.

"Was it for anything special?"

Mr Bear shook his head. He was looking outside
at the faraway trees where the magpie lived.
"We have to go there," he said. "Otherwise
there'll be no cake."

So Mr Bear and Small Bear
set off to find the magpie.
It was a long way.

First Mr Bear
and Small Bear
had to cross
the boggy
marsh.

Then they had to
clamber up to the top
of the rocky ridge . . .

. . . and down the other side.

And finally, they had
to pick a path through
the dark woods

until they came

to where

the magpie

lived.

The bird was tidying his nest.

"What do you want?" he cawed.

"Can't you see I'm busy?"

"See that boring bit of metal you've just found?"
said Mr Bear. "The dull and unimportant little cog."

"What about it?" scolded the magpie.
"What'll you give me for it?"
Mr Bear nearly groaned out loud.
He hadn't thought to bring any money.
"Come on," insisted the magpie.
"I want shiny, sparkly stuff . . . "
"Look," said Small Bear, holding out
her tinsel crown. "Will this do?"

The magpie's eyes grew wide.
"I'll say," he shrieked. "Here,
swap you." And dropping the cog
to the ground, he swooped down and plucked
Small Bear's crown out of her hands
and flew off, cackling delightedly.
"WELL DONE!" said Mr Bear.
"Hoorah for Small Bear."
And back they went to the mill
with the cog for Mr Grizzle-Bear.

Through
the dark
woods . . .

up and down the
rocky ridge . . .

back through the swamp . . .
and finally,

just as the first stars
were coming out,
back to the mill . . .

. . . where all was still, silent and closed for the night.
"Oh no!" wailed Small Bear, and she began to cry.
"Never mind," said Mr Bear, minding very much
indeed. "Let's go home and see what Mummy's
made for birthday supper, shall we?"

But when they reached home,
the lights were off and the house
was in darkness.

"Oh, NO," groaned Mr Bear, close to tears,
as he opened the front door. "This is the
worst birthday of my whole . . ."

"SURPRISE!"

"HAPPY BIRTHDAY, Mr Bear."